Mummies Around the World

the BIG PICTURE

CAPSTONE PRESS
a capstone imprint

Anna Claybourne

First Facts is published by Capstone Press, a Capstone imprint,
151 Good Counsel Drive, P.O. Box 669, Mankato, Minnesota 56002.
www.capstonepub.com

First published in 2010 by A&C Black Publishers Limited, 36 Soho Square, London W1D 3QY
www.acblack.com
Copyright © A&C Black Ltd. 2010

Produced for A&C Black by Calcium. www.calciumcreative.co.uk

062011
006273

Library of Congress Cataloging-in-Publication Data
Claybourne, Anna.
  Mummies around the world / by Anna Claybourne.
    p. cm. – (First facts, the big picture)
  Includes bibliographical references and index.
  ISBN 978-1-4296-5513-2 (library binding)
  ISBN 978-1-4296-5523-1 (paperback)
  1. Mummies–Juvenile literature. I. Title. II. Series.

GN293.C58 2011
393'.3–dc22   2010013410

Acknowledgements

The publishers would like to thank the following for their kind permission to reproduce their photographs:

Cover: Fotolia: Sam Shapiro; Shutterstock: Fatih Kocyildir (front), Wikimedia Commons: Linda Spashett (back).
Pages: Corbis: Dave Bartruff 14; Fotolia: Sam Shapiro 6, 19; Getty Images: Robert Harding World Imagery 20,
Stone/Art Wolfe 11; Istockphoto: Rescigno Floriano 24; Photographers Direct: Robin Weaver 16; Rex Features:
12; Shutterstock: Galyna Andrushko 10-11, Carlos Arguelles 18-19, Vaju Ariel 5, Bond Girl 1, Amanda Haddox 3,
12-13, Xie HangXing 20-21, Mirek Hejnicki 8-9 (background), Fatih Kocyildir 6-7, 8-9, Evgeny Kovalev SPB 16-17,
Giancarlo Liguori 4-5, Juriah Mosin 22-23, Tito Wong 14-15; Wikimedia Commons: E. Michael Smith 18,
Linda Spashett 7, Ranveig Thattai 2-3.

Contents

Mummies!

When people die, their bodies usually **rot away**. A mummy is a dead body that does not rot.

Mummy makers

A long time ago, people learned how to preserve a body by turning it into a mummy.

Dead famous

Tutankhamun is the most famous mummy ever.

4

Another world

People made mummies because they believed the dead went to another world and would need their bodies there.

Perfect Mummy

The Egyptians made the most famous mummies ever! They spent 70 days making each one.

What a job!

First, the mummy makers took out the body's insides. They covered the body in salt to stop it from rotting. Then they **stuffed** it.

Mummies were wrapped in strips of cloth.

Looking good

An Egyptian mummy was put in a **coffin** with a beautiful, painted mask over its face.

How do I look?

Mummy Home

The Egyptians built wonderful tombs for important mummies, such as kings and queens.

Amazing pyramids

Some mummy tombs are huge buildings shaped like a triangle. These buildings are called pyramids.

8

Valley of Kings

Some tombs were cut into the rock.
Many Egyptian kings were buried
in rock tombs in a place called
the Valley of the Kings in Egypt.

*Pharaoh Khufu's
pyramid, center,
is the tallest of all.*

Mummy valley

Shrunken Heads

Could you wear a head as a necklace? The Jivaro Indians of Ecuador once did!

Battle trophies

The Jivaro took their enemies' heads in battle. They **shrunk** the heads and sewed them shut to keep the enemies' spirits from doing harm.

Head necklace

Shrinking heads

To shrink heads, the Jivaro removed the skulls. They placed the heads in hot water, then dried them with hot air.

Today the Jivaro people wear bead necklaces!

Mummy Man!

Who would want to be a mummy? Jeremy Bentham did! He lived in England about 200 years ago.

Make me a mummy

Jeremy Bentham was a **scientist** who was fascinated by mummies—he even asked to be turned into one when he died!

Jeremy's mummy can still be seen on display today.

Head case

Jeremy's head was put on display with his body. But when students stole the head and played tricks with it, a wax one was made instead!

Mummy mad!

Still Alive

Some Buddhist priests in Japan turned themselves into mummies!

Living mummies

The priests ate tree **bark** and drank tree **sap** tea. They knew the **poisons** in the bark and tea would kill them, but would also stop their bodies from rotting when they died.

This Buddhist priest mummy can be seen in Thailand.

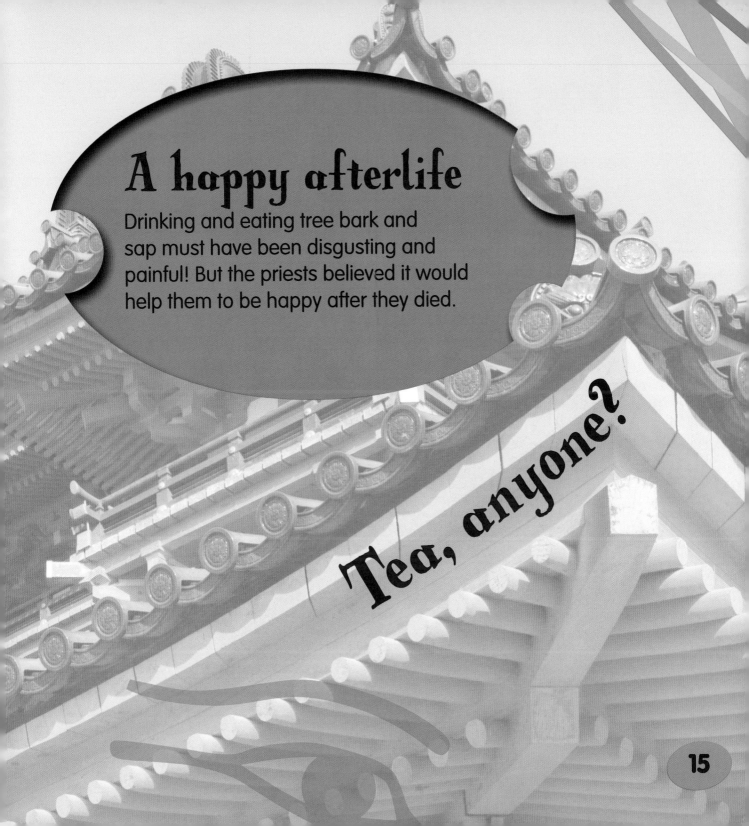

A happy afterlife

Drinking and eating tree bark and sap must have been disgusting and painful! But the priests believed it would help them to be happy after they died.

Tea, anyone?

Bog Mummies

Some people became mummies when they fell into a bog!

Body story

Some bog bodies were put there on purpose. People were sometimes killed and then thrown into a bog. The body then turned into a mummy.

A mummy that was found in a bog

In a pickle

Bog water is a little like the vinegar used to make pickles. A body in the water will get pickled!

Bogged down

Animals Too

Did you know that there are even animal mummies too?

Pet mummies

The Egyptians thought cats were special. They even turned them into mummies and buried them with their dead owners!

The Egyptians turned dogs into mummies too.

Mummy zoo

The Egyptians also turned birds, crocodiles, monkeys, cows, and even hippos into mummies.

Perfect pet

Dead Rich

The Egyptians buried things with their mummies.

Still need it

The Egyptians believed their mummies would need food, tools, and clothes in the next world. They buried them with the mummy.

Wonderful treasure, such as this gold statue, was buried with mummies.

Not lonely

Servant statues were buried with the mummies of important people. The Egyptians believed the dead would need servants in the next life.

Treasure chest

Glossary

bark rough covering on a tree

bog a place full of watery soil

Buddhist priests people who believe in and serve a god called Buddha

coffin a special box in which a body is buried

poison a substance that can kill or harm someone

rot to make or become rotten

sap sticky juice inside a tree

scientist a person who studies things to find out how they work

shrunk made smaller

stuffed to fill a dead body with material that keeps the body stiff

tombs buildings in which bodies are buried

Further Reading

FactHound offers a safe, fun way to find Internet sites related to this book. All of the sites on FactHound have been researched by our staff.

Here's all you do:

Visit www.facthound.com

FactHound will fetch the best sites for you!

Books

Freaky Facts About Mummies by Iqbal Hussain, Two Can Publishing (2006).

Mummies by Elizabeth Carney, National Geographic (2009).

Mummies by Kremena Spengler, Capstone Press (2009).

Index